Naughty STORIES for Good boys and girls

CHRISTOPHER MILNE

An Upside-Down Boy
and Other Naughty Stories for Good Boys and Girls
published in 2010 by
Hardie Grant Egmont
85 High Street
Prahran, Victoria 3181, Australia
www.hardiegrantegmont.com.au

PEFC
PEFC/21-31-16

The pages of this book are printed on paper derived
from forests promoting sustainable management.

All rights reserved. No part of this publication may be reproduced,
stored in a retrieval system or transmitted in any form by any means
without the prior permission of the publishers and copyright owner.

A CiP record for this title is available from the National Library of Australia.

Text copyright © 2010 Christopher Milne
Illustration and design copyright © 2010 Hardie Grant Egmont

Illustration and design by Simon Swingler
Typesetting by Ektavo
Printed in Australia

1 3 5 7 9 10 8 6 4 2

Other books by Christopher Milne
The Day Our Teacher Went Mad and Other Naughty Stories
The Bravest Kid I've Ever Known and Other Naughty Stories
The Girl Who Blew Up Her Brother and Other Naughty Stories

Also available from www.christophermilne.com.au
The Western Sydney Kid
Little Johnnie and the Naughty Boat People

an
upside
down
boy

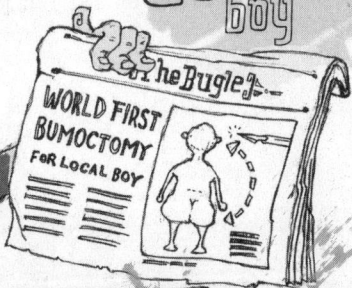

The Bugle

WORLD FIRST
BUMOCTOMY
FOR LOCAL BOY

24

-AND-
OTHER

Naughty
STORIES for
Good boys and girls

CHRISTOPHER MILNE

Illustrations by
Simon Swingler

hardie grant EGMONT

TO PETE AND ROB

Peter and Robert are my two sons and they
provided the inspiration for most of my stories.
They have always been a bit naughty in
real life, but also brave, clever, decent
and funny — and much-loved.

Pete and Rob went to Nayook Primary School
and many of these stories are loosely
based on those wonderful years.

Christopher McC... (signature)

contents

an upside down boy

Poor little Jason Grant was born with his face where his bottom should be, and his bottom where his face should be. Which is not the best way to start out in life.

His mum said she still loved him very much and that it didn't matter what anyone else might think. She thought he had a beautiful little face. **Or bottom.**

1

Unfortunately, not everyone felt the same way. Especially Jason's grandma. She was so embarrassed that she used to hold Jason upside-down, so his face was on top.

Jason's mum was really angry with her. 'What's wrong with you?' she screamed. 'So what if Jason's a bit different? None of us is perfect. Some people have big ears, others have bent noses. Jason just happens to have a face that looks a bit like a bottom.'

Poor Grandma. After that she tried to do the right thing. But just as she was getting used to the idea, she turned around quickly to thank Jason for a Christmas present and kissed him right on the butt.

The other kids at kindergarten didn't care. As long as Jason shared his lollies and was good at playing games, what did it matter how he looked?

Clothes were a bit of a problem. But only for a while. Other mums soon realised that old pairs of pants with holes in the bottom were no good anymore for their own kids, but perfect for Jason.

Unfortunately, as Jason grew older, life started to change. He noticed that kids he didn't know seemed to stare all the time. Then a whole lot of nasty jokes went around the neighbourhood. And then it was time for him to start school. What would that be like?

Jason always found a way
to do what kids do best...

4

Grandma said to his mum, 'You're not going to send him to a normal school, are you?'

'Why not?' asked Jason's mum, getting really angry again. 'He's a person, isn't he? He can read and write and run and speak the same as anyone else!'

'What if he's standing up,' said Jason's grandma, 'and the teacher asks him to sit down? He won't be able to see!'

Jason's mum couldn't answer that one.

Well, Jason did start school. And although everyone was nice to him, and he handled the schoolwork well enough, he felt lonely. Terribly lonely. It seemed that the other kids were only being nice because they felt sorry

for him. And that can be an awful feeling.

Poor Jason. He tried to make proper friends with the kids who played lunchtime footy, but he got too many frees – every tackle was head-high. So Jason played by himself. He felt as if he didn't have a single friend in the whole world.

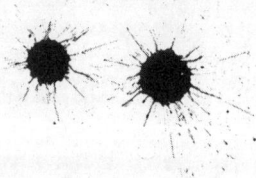

One day, a new girl started at school. Her name was Cindy Cooper.

'What are you sooking about?' she asked.

'I'm not sooking,' said Jason.

'Yes, you are,' said Cindy. 'I've watched

you. Other kids ask you to play and you say no. Because you think they feel sorry for you. But they don't. It's just you feeling sorry for yourself. You're nothing but a big cry-baby.'

Jason couldn't believe it. Who did this stupid girl think she was? How dare she speak to him like that!

Jason seriously thought about punching her out. Trouble was, he knew she was right. And much as he hated to admit it, he thought he might like her.

So, what's the best way to tell a girl you like her? Tell her you don't like her!

The very next day, Jason looked hard at

Cindy to find as many faults as he could. She had rather a large face, he decided, and slightly sticky-out ears.

'Hey, boofhead,' he called. 'You've left your doors open.'

'At least my head points the right way, Bumface,' replied Cindy.

'I'm not surprised it points the right way,' said Jason. 'It just has to follow that nose of yours. I've seen smaller conks on an elephant.'

And so they went, piling it on each other for a full hour. Finally, neither of them could think of another thing to say. Then, just as they went to walk away, Jason

called out, 'Hey, there's something else…
I think I like you.'

'And I like you, too,' said Cindy.

After that, Jason and Cindy were never
apart. They mucked around together before
school, after school and, much to the teacher's
displeasure, during school.

It was as if no-one else in the world existed.
As if they could see inside each other.

What they saw on the outside hardly
mattered at all. Like plain wrapping around
a beautiful present.

And so it was until a terrible, terrible day
came. A day Jason tried very hard to forget.

Cindy walked straight up to him and

said, 'Jason, I want you to be strong. You know how my dad works for a bank? Well, he's been shifted. We've *all* been shifted. Interstate. Jason, I won't be around anymore.'

For a long time, Jason just looked at her. He didn't say anything. Then he looked away and began to cry. Hopelessly.

A week later, as Cindy drove away, she called out, 'I'll be back, Jason. One day. I promise. I really like you.'

Jason's world had ended. That was *it* as far as he was concerned. No Cindy, no nothing. Back to being a loser. A loser with no friends. A freak.

Jason couldn't get Cindy out of his mind. He even thought back to how they'd met. How she had called him a cry-baby for feeling sorry for himself.

Suddenly, it came to him. Isn't that just what he was doing all over again? Feeling sorry for himself? How stupid. Cindy, who he'd liked and trusted so much, had taught him the best lesson in life and he'd forgotten it already! He felt ashamed.

So from that day on, Jason woke up every morning and told himself, 'I will not be a cry-baby today.'

And do you know what? He started to feel better. School wasn't so boring anymore

and people were somehow nicer. Jason even made some new friends, too.

But he never forgot Cindy.

The years went by and Jason did well at school and lived the best life he could as an upside-down boy.

Then one day his mother said she wanted to talk to him. She'd met a doctor who said that lots of new things had been discovered over the years, and that it might be possible for Jason to have an operation. That his bottom could be swapped with his face to make him the right way up.

A bumoctomy, it was called.

Jason wasn't too sure what he wanted. It would be nice to be the right way up, but he'd become used to the way he was. The thought of changing scared him.

The doctor visited Jason the next day and talked to him about the operation. 'It's a brand-new procedure,' said the doctor, 'and it would make you famous. It would be in all the papers!'

And so it was. The very next day, the headlines said:

WORLD-FIRST BUMOCTOMY FOR LOCAL BOY.

And Jason hadn't even said yes yet!

That night Jason tossed and turned and turned and tossed. What should he do?

In the morning, he felt as if he hadn't had any sleep at all. And then there was a knock at the door.

It'll be that doctor again, thought Jason.

'There's someone to see you,' said his mum.

'I know,' sighed Jason.

As he walked into the lounge room to speak to the doctor, he felt lonelier than he'd ever felt in his whole life. He had to decide about the operation all by himself. Even though his mum and dad had spoken to him heaps about it, they said that in the end, it was up to him.

But it wasn't the doctor who stood there in the lounge room. It was someone else. Someone he hadn't seen for six long years.

It was Cindy.

'Told you I'd be back,' said Cindy. 'While I was coming here on the train I read about you in the papers. I don't want you to change. I love you exactly as you are. I'm back, Jason. And I'm never going to leave you again.'

the boy who said too many rude words

Simon Kemp was always getting into trouble for swearing. But this time it was serious.

'Uses far too many rude words,' said his school report.

Simon's oldies chucked a mental over his report and told his teachers they could expect an improvement. A BIG one.

Simon did improve. You see, his dad said that unless his swearing stopped completely, he could forget about going to the football for a whole year. And that, for Simon Kemp, a mad St Kilda supporter, was simply unthinkable.

So, every time Simon went to say a rude word, he stopped, took a deep breath and said to himself, 'St Kilda.' And it worked. Fantastically well.

Until one very unlucky day.

Simon was doing some jobs for the lady next door, Mrs Forbes. Simon hated working for Mrs Forbes, but he had no choice. His dad made him do it. Every second Sunday.

Usually it was weeding, but sometimes stuff like painting or fixing her fence. Simon had to work for six hours and always for free.

'It's the neighbourly thing to do,' said Dad. 'Especially with Mrs Forbes being so old.'

Doesn't stop her going to bingo, thought Simon. *Wish she'd cark it.*

Anyway, if it was so neighbourly, why didn't his dad help the old hag?

The main reason Simon hated working for Mrs Forbes was that she never, ever said thank you. Not once. And nothing was ever good enough.

'You've missed a bit there,' she'd say. Or, 'You'll have to do that again.'

Maybe if I weed the vegie patch really well, thought Simon, *the carrots will grow bigger and she'll choke on one.*

And another thing about Mrs Forbes — she never, ever stopped giving Simon a hard time about his manners.

'It really is time you started to improve yourself,' Mrs Forbes would say. 'Going to church like me would be a good start.'

How can I go to church? thought Simon. *I'm stuck here doing your stupid garden.*

One particular Sunday, Simon was fixing the fence where it had been broken by one of Mrs Forbes's dopey trees. It was a hot day and Simon was tired. Just as he banged in the last nail, the hammer slipped from his hand, fell, and landed right on his toe.

OUCH!

The pain was something terrible. But Simon took a deep breath, calmly leant down, held his toe, and said, 'St Kilda.'

As he stood up, however, he banged his head a **ripper** on a tree branch. 'St Kilda,' said Simon again, gritting his teeth.

And you'll never guess, as Simon hopped out from under the tree, with one hand on his head, the other holding his toe, he stubbed his other foot on a pointy rock.

This time Simon didn't look down calmly. Nor did he take a very deep breath.

Instead, he looked to the sky, clenched his fists and screamed, 'Stuff St Kilda! Crap, poo, wee, snot and BUM!'

Poor Simon couldn't have chosen a worse time. Walking towards him, having just returned from church, was Mrs Forbes.

When Mrs Forbes heard Simon's words, she almost fainted. She slumped onto a seat, fanned herself and said, 'May God have mercy on your soul.'

You can imagine the carry-on after that. Mrs Forbes went straight to Simon's parents and told them everything.

Simon received a smacked bottom, no tea and, just as his dad had threatened, no football for a year.

When it came time for St Kilda's first game of the season, Simon sat in his room and cried. He couldn't even bear to listen to it on the radio.

The next week, he thought to himself, *I know what, I'll pretend I'm there.*

He turned the radio up full-blast, put on his St Kilda jumper with number twelve for Nick Riewoldt on the back, microwaved a pie with sauce and waved his flogger.

But it wasn't the same. Not at all. Even the pie tasted different. Simon Kemp turned off the radio, lay on his bed, whispered, 'Go Saints,' and cried into his pillow.

The week following, Simon thought, *This is crazy. I'm going to go mad if I don't stop thinking about footy. I'll do something else! I'll read a book.*

Trouble was, most of Simon's books were about football, so, in desperation, he looked at his mum and dad's bookshelf. The first book he pulled out was called *The Joy of Sex.*

How disgusting, thought Simon. *At their age!*

Then one book happened to catch his eye – *How to Forget Your Worries.*

I've got worries, thought Simon.

Some of the words were a bit big but Simon really enjoyed it. It talked about the power of our minds and how we can train ourselves to think only about good stuff, instead of worrying about things we can't change.

But the bit that really got him was about mind control. That's when one person can put ideas into someone else's mind, just by thinking about them. It's as though the message travels through the air, like a TV signal. Some people believe in it, others don't. Some people are good at it, others aren't.

As it turned out, Simon Kemp was very, very good at mind control. In no time, he had his dog and cat doing all sorts of tricks, just by thinking about them.

But Simon had bigger fish in mind. An old flathead called Mrs Forbes.

The very next Sunday, Simon said to his mum and dad that perhaps Mrs Forbes was right after all. That he really did need to improve himself.

If they didn't mind, he had decided to go to church today.

'I can't believe it,' said his dad.

At church, Simon said hello to Mrs Forbes, but she refused to even speak to him.

Good, thought Simon.

Inside the church, Simon waited for Mrs Forbes to find a seat. Then, without her noticing, he sneaked up and sat right behind her. Staring straight into the back of Mrs Forbes's head, Simon started thinking some very naughty thoughts.

Terrible thoughts.

And they worked.

Mrs Forbes started shifting in her seat and looking worried. She coughed awkwardly and became quite pink in the cheeks as she suddenly realised she was about to do and say something unthinkable. Which made her even pinker.

Suddenly, in front of one hundred of her best church friends, Mrs Forbes stood up and yelled, 'Cop this!'

And let go one of the **loudest smells**

you could ever imagine.

Well, do you think that didn't cause a stir? People just couldn't believe it. Mrs Forbes! Of course, Mrs Forbes couldn't believe it herself. But that wasn't all.

As the new vicar walked in, Mrs Forbes nudged the lady next to her and said, 'He's got a **nice bum**.'

'Oh, how crude!' said the lady next to her. 'Mrs Forbes, I don't know what's going on with you today, but I really do believe it's time you left.'

'Oh yeah?' said Mrs Forbes, 'Why don't you rack off yourself!'

Simon didn't ever use his mind control again. He thought he'd had more than his fair

share of fun, just in that one day. Poor Mrs Forbes didn't go back to church for ages. In fact, she was banned until the doctor said she was well again.

And Simon certainly hasn't been back to church. No place for a boy like him. Too many rude words.

the mad gambler

Claire Troupe loved gambling. Betting on things. To the point where it drove us all mad.

'I bet I'm taller than you,' she would say. 'I bet you two pieces of chocolate I know what's in your lunchbox. I bet you four pieces of chocolate that my mum and dad earn more than yours do.'

Tell someone who cares, Claire!

Get a life!

We never understood why Claire was so into betting on things. Maybe it was her way of getting attention? Perhaps she was bored? Whatever.

For a long time, Claire's betting was, as I say, a pain in the butt. But it was never more than that, until suddenly everything changed. Claire started to bet with money. And stupidly – don't ask me how – the rest of us got sucked in, too.

It all started with Claire's eleventh birthday, when her parents couldn't decide

what to buy her. Instead they gave her **one hundred lovely dollars**.

The feel, the smell, the look of the money affected her. It weaved a spell. She couldn't stop thinking about it. She wanted more. How to get it? Gambling. Gambling with a little bit of cheating! Just enough to win every time.

Well, not every time. Not at first, anyway. You see, for Claire to make money she had to get it out of us and the way she did it was very clever indeed. Guess who was her first target? Dopey me.

Claire walked up at lunchtime during a muck-around game of netball and said, 'I'll bet you a dollar that I can beat you shooting goals. Best of ten.'

'Rack off,' I replied.

'Scared you might lose?' Claire said. 'Beat me and you'll have two dollars. Unless you think you're not good enough.'

Now, it so happened that I knew Claire was useless at netball. Useless at most things, as a matter of fact. And by now, everyone was starting to gather around.

I'd look like a wuss, I supposed, if I said no. 'OK,' I said. 'Best out of ten.'

Well, it wasn't even a contest. Me, seven. Clare nothing. Money for jam. Claire tried the same with the other kids and lost again! What a dork. What a loser!

It was a funny feeling, suddenly having that extra dollar for free. Sure, a buck isn't that

much, I suppose, but there was something special about it. Something magic. As if the world was being nice to me. As if I deserved it.

So, when Claire asked the following day if I'd like to play again, I quickly said yes. You won't be surprised to learn that I won again. Thank you very much.

None of us felt that bad about taking Claire's money. She deserved it, didn't she? Driving us mad all the time with, 'I'll bet you this. I'll bet you that.' Who knew, it might even make her stop.

It was about a week later when Claire said she was sick of losing all the time, and that it was only fair if we played something else.

'How about cards?' she asked. 'We both

flip a card and the highest wins.'

'Fair enough,' I said. Even if I lost this one time, I was still going to be in front.

I lost.

'Another,' said Claire.

'Can't,' I said. 'A dollar's all I have.'

'Tomorrow,' said Claire.

'Maybe,' I replied.

Of course, 'maybe' became 'yes'. I wanted that feeling of winning again.

I lost.

By the end of the week, Claire had most of the school flipping cards, and, slowly but surely, every last dollar of Claire's lost netball money returned to her.

But I was smarter than Claire because

I knew that winning at gambling was really just luck. I was lucky at netball. Claire was lucky at cards. Now it was my turn again, and it made me excited.

The trouble was, every other kid in school, it seemed, was thinking exactly the same thing. It wasn't long before Claire had us betting on anything that moved. Snails crawling up a wall, whether or not Mr Trainor would crack a wobbly that day, who would be the first to scream **'stop!'** if Carla Zotti scratched her fingernails down the blackboard, who could chew silver paper for the longest, who had the most freckles, who could crack their knuckles the loudest, who had the worst breath and who did that smell during religious instruction.

Gambling fever, it was. Some of us could think of nothing else. Which meant two things. Claire – who was usually cheating by suggesting we bet on things to which she already knew the answers – was getting very rich. And others, like me, were getting into very big trouble. Borrowing money, owing money to Claire and, eventually, having to sell stuff to her. If we didn't pay her back, she threatened to give Gail 'Gorilla' Golan ten bucks to bash us up.

Yet although Claire was making heaps, it wasn't making her happy.

There's really no such thing as winning at gambling, she secretly thought to herself.

As soon as you do win, you just want to gamble

again. No win is ever big enough.

Which made Claire angry. She felt cheated.

Who could she blame? Us, of course.

So Claire started to punish us by making us look like fools. Humiliating us. Which, of course, made us hate Claire, which, in turn, made her worse.

Then it happened. Poor little Amy Than owed Claire twenty dollars and she had nothing left to sell.

'OK,' said Claire. 'I bet you twenty dollars you haven't got the guts to climb onto the roof and bust a piece off the school TV antenna.'

'All right,' said Amy, with Gorilla Golan leering at her in the background. 'I will.'

Poor Amy didn't even get to the antenna. It had been raining and Amy slipped on the roof, shot over the guttering and fell screaming towards the concrete.

She would surely have been badly hurt or even killed, except for one very good piece of luck — she landed on something soft. **Claire's face.**

Claire spent the rest of her life with a nose like a squashed mango. I'd bet that didn't make her happy.

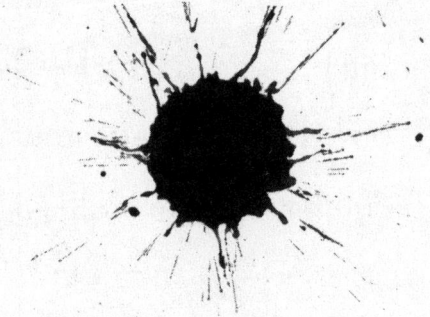

a very lonely boy

Little Kenny was a lonely boy. A very lonely boy. He had no friends at all. Unless you counted Boof, his dog. No-one could say Boof hadn't been the best dog-friend a kid had ever had. But Boof was getting old. And his days of playing with Kenny for hours on end were over.

Poor old Boof – he'd see Kenny playing by himself and he knew he should be dropping a stick for Kenny to throw. But his legs just wouldn't take him very far anymore. If Kenny turned around, Boof's eyes would say 'stick' and his tail would wag, but that was as far as it went. Sometimes it made Kenny cry.

One cold, windy day, Kenny was outside mucking around in the dirt making secret tunnels for some old toy soldiers. And much as he tried not to, he started – for what seemed like the thousandth time – to think about why he was such a loser. That's what Derek 'Fierce' Pierce called him, anyway.

He knew that part of the reason was his

mum and dad not being together anymore, but he didn't want to think about that too much because it made him even sadder.

You see, Kenny and his mum had shifted to the country with his grandma, leaving Dad in the city. Dad, who he loved so much and now hardly ever saw.

At least in the city he'd had one good mate. Stinky Anderson. Stinky had had an accident on the first day of school and the name had stuck ever since.

But the biggest reason for Kenny's loneliness was a feeling that somehow, he never fitted in anywhere. And once you feel that, then other kids feel it too. And

pretty soon you don't fit in. And then you say, 'See, I was right.' It was partly because Kenny secretly blamed himself for his parents splitting up. It wasn't his fault, of course. It never is. But it made Kenny feel bad about himself and that's when everything seemed to go so wrong.

There was something else, too – the sort of games Kenny used to like. 'Wussy games,' some kids would call them. Stuff where you have to think and pretend. Like building dirt castles and having make-believe wars where the bad guys get their heads blown off and guts spurt out of their necks. And collecting lizards and seeing if they die or not.

The other kids in this country town weren't into dopey stuff like that. They were into grown-up things like cricket and hanging around the milk bar.

Kenny's mum used to ask kids home to play, but somehow they always had excuses for not coming over. Kenny said it didn't matter because he was really happy being with his mum.

And if his mum tried to arrange for Kenny to go to other kids' places, Kenny would say he felt sick. Secretly, he couldn't stand the thought of getting there and not fitting in.

So, Kenny played by himself. Before school, after school, on weekends and on holidays. With sad, smelly Boof looking on. And the wind blew and Kenny's face grew sadder.

His beautiful little face was freckled, with crooked teeth and the loneliest eyes in the world.

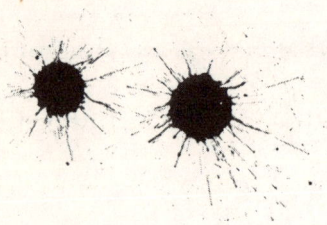

Fierce Pierce was the first one to notice that something was going on.

'What do you reckon that loser Kenny's doing in his backyard?' he asked his mate Fridge. 'Every morning when I go past on the way to school, there's more dirt. In a pile.

Heaps of it.'

'A swimming pool?' wondered Fridge.

Fierce thought not. Surely they'd get a bulldozer or something for that.

'Perhaps he's burying food?' suggested Fridge. From a stupid suggestion like that, you can probably guess how Fridge got his name. Fierce didn't even bother to answer.

So, the very next morning Fierce went straight up to Kenny and said, 'Hey loser, what's with all the dirt?'

'Oh, nothing,' said little Kenny.

Kenny would have gladly told Fierce, but he thought Fierce might laugh. You see, Kenny was building the most excellent underground cubby house the world had ever seen – for himself and some pretend friends. But how do you admit you're so lonely you have to have pretend friends?

'What do you mean, nothing?' said Fierce.

Kenny could tell Fierce was going to punch him out if he didn't give a good answer. So he lied. 'Mum's making me do it. For pocket money. She's going to plant some trees.'

Fierce looked hard at Kenny. Fierce knew how cruel parents could be – making you work for pocket money – but he wasn't sure if he believed Kenny or not. But the bell went, so Kenny got away with it. For the time being.

You should have seen the cubby. It started with a secret entrance hidden behind some bushes and then went straight down into a big dark room. Kenny had candles burning in the corners.

Kenny's dad had shown him how to build safe cubbies, and somehow every spadeful of dirt, every heavy bucketful tipped on the pile, was for his dad. Maybe one day Dad would come to visit again and Kenny could show him what a good job he'd done.

From the main dark room, two tunnels headed off in different directions. If you weren't a member of the cubby club, you wouldn't know which was the right one and

that was something that definitely needed to be known. One went to the secret chamber, and the other to a hole full of the **worst, slimiest,** stinkiest, **pooiest** water you could ever imagine.

'Boof's hole,' Kenny called it. 'Boof's bones and business hole' would have been a better description. Kenny didn't just put Boof's bones there, though. He swapped them for big bits of spare steak from the fridge. The business came free of charge.

From the secret chamber, there were two more tunnels. One led to the food and drinks cave, and the other to a fantastic underground maze.

If you could find your way through the maze — and only cubby members would know how — you finally reached the most secret of secret places. **The star chamber.**

Kenny would never tell what was in the star chamber, but to have built such an excellent maze it must have been something good. Really good.

So, the days passed, and then weeks, and finally, Fierce couldn't help but ask again. 'Hey, misery guts. What's happened to those trees your mum was putting in?'

'She hasn't got them yet,' lied Kenny. 'I made the holes a bit big so she's got to wait for them to grow.'

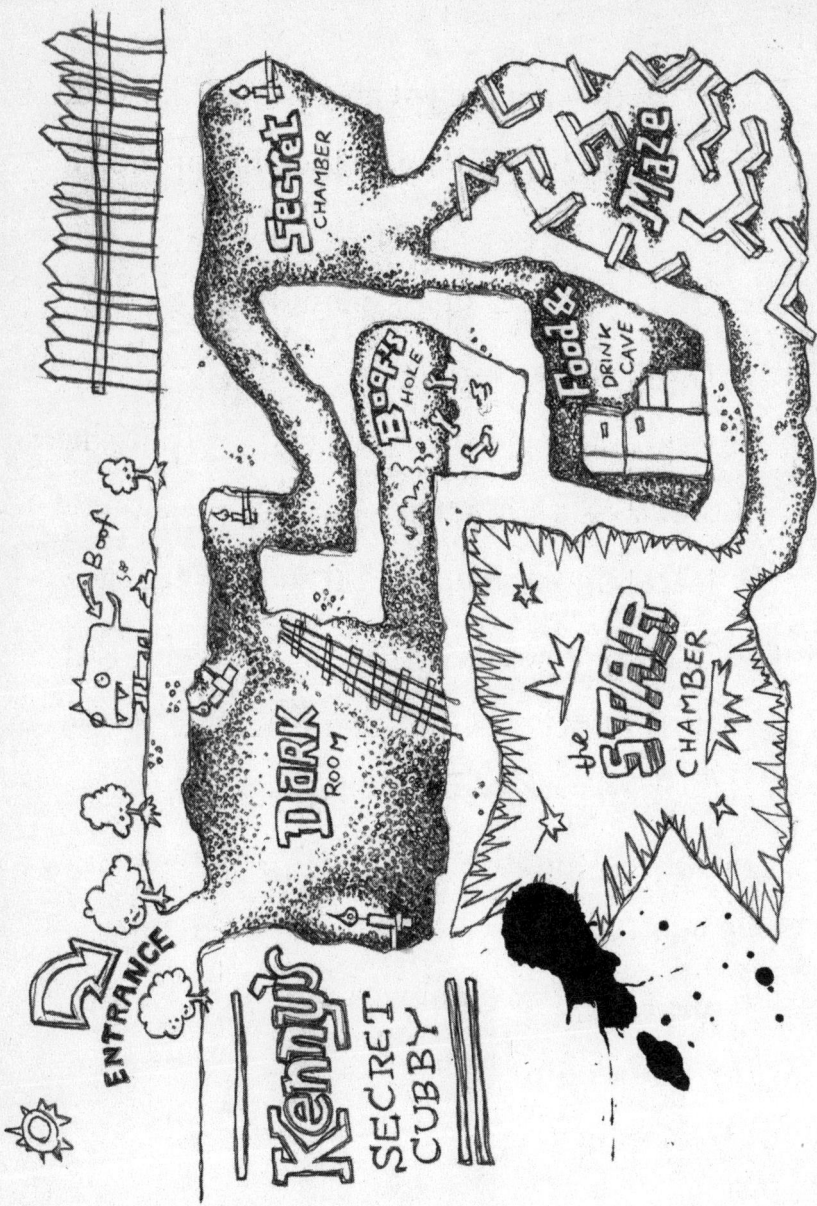

Secret Chamber

THE MAZE

Boof's Hole

Food & Drink Cave

the STAR CHAMBER

DARK ROOM

ENTRANCE

Boof

Kenny's SECRET CUBBY

This time Fierce got angry. 'Bull,' he said. And he pushed Kenny in the chest. 'You're lying.'

'No, I'm not,' said Kenny.

By this time kids were starting to gather around. They loved to watch a fight. Especially if they weren't in it.

'Tell me the truth or I'll smash your face in,' said Fierce.

Given the choice, thought Kenny, *I'd rather not have my face smashed in.* So he took a deep breath and got himself as ready as possible to be laughed at.

'It's a secret cubby house,' said Kenny. 'For me and my friends.'

'What friends?' asked Fierce.

'Pretend ones,' said Kenny.

'Pretend ones!' said Fierce. 'What a dork! What a loser!'

And sure enough, the kids all laughed their heads off. Cacked themselves. But not for nearly as long as Kenny expected. And, in a strange way, although the kids did laugh a fair bit, Kenny didn't care. At least now it was all over.

But that's where Kenny was wrong. It wasn't all over. Not at all. You see, kids started talking. It was the word 'secret' that got them going. As Kenny's mum said, there's nothing country people like better than discovering a good secret.

And then the rumours started. One rumour said that Kenny was building a huge grave for Boof – what with Boof looking like he was going to cark it any day now.

Another said Kenny was working as a spy and it was really an underground nuclear reactor. Whatever it was, almost every kid in school decided he just had to know.

So, one night after school, Fierce and twenty-six of his mates knocked on Kenny's door and said if he didn't show them his cubby, **they'd bash his brains out.** Luckily, Kenny's mum was listening, so she went to the door and said, 'You must be Fierce.'

'Yeah,' said Fierce. 'So what?'

'So why don't you all come inside?' said Kenny's mum. 'I've got loads of boxes of chocolate left over from Easter and plenty of lemonade in the fridge. No point in bashing Kenny's brains out on an empty stomach.'

Fierce was so surprised by this that suddenly all his toughness seemed to leave him. 'OK,' said Fierce. 'Thanks.'

So, including Kenny, twenty-eight kids sat down and gutsed themselves sick. After that, no-one felt like bashing anyone's brains out. And slowly and strangely, Kenny started to feel good. It mightn't have been for the best of reasons, but for the first time in so long he didn't feel lonely.

And then the suggestions started. 'Hey, Kenny,' said one kid. 'How 'bout we have a muck around in your cubby?'

'Sure,' said Kenny, 'But parts of it are dangerous – very dangerous – so I'd better show you a map first. And to be allowed in at all, you have to be a member. Do you all want to join?'

'Yeah!' the kids all shouted.

So, quietly and carefully, Kenny showed the kids how to pick the right tunnels, how not to fall into Boof's hole and how to get through the maze to the most secret of secret places. The star chamber.

And everyone loved it.

Somehow, because Kenny had been lonely for so long and because he'd had to use his imagination so much, Kenny had a knack for making things sound exciting. Really exciting. It wasn't so much what he said, but the way he said it. Even Fierce secretly thought that he could just sit there and listen to Kenny forever.

There was this look in Kenny's eyes which made it seem as though he knew things the other kids could never know – as though he'd been to a place they didn't even know existed. And when Kenny said, 'OK, is everyone ready?' kids just sat there and waited for him to say something else. Never in their lives had they realised that telling stories and stuff could be so much fun. Almost as good as mud fights.

Fierce and his mates thought the cubby was so excellent. 'Radical,' they said.

From that day on, Kenny just knew he would never be without friends again. Because the kids had come to him. He wasn't fitting in, exactly – it was just that everything felt OK. And if you feel OK, making friends is easy.

Now, what was or wasn't in the star chamber will never be known because only members were allowed in. And one of the

rules of membership was that you had to keep things secret. At one time a rumour went around that Kenny had discovered gold down there and was waiting till he was older so the government didn't take it. Who knows, could be true.

As little Kenny watched his new friends playing in the cubby one day, he walked over to the spot where he used to play with toy soldiers. He smiled, and thought to himself that he'd never felt happier in his life. He was even going down to see his dad every second weekend.

Poor old Boof eventually passed away. Kenny and his mum had a little funeral for him and buried Boof with his favourite stick and the blanket he slept on as a puppy.

Kenny cried during the funeral, but it wasn't so much because of Boof. It was because twenty-seven members of the cubby club turned up to support him.

the boy who lived in a dunny

Tony Boyd had woken up in a sooky-baby mood and it was only a matter of time before he made a jerk of himself. Before he said something he would later regret.

Tony knew he was headed for trouble, but it didn't stop him. He punched his little brother Gary on the arm, kicked yesterday's jocks under the bed, refused to eat breakfast, left toothpaste spray on the mirror, swore at the dog and said there was no way he would be eating the fish-paste sandwiches his mum had made for lunch.

'They smell like an armpit,' he said loudly.

And that's where the trouble began. Tony's father had just walked into the kitchen and said that if Tony didn't say sorry to his mother for that last remark, he would pull down his pants and smack his butt.

Tony knew that when his father threatened a whack it hardly ever happened, but it definitely did mean something bad was on the cards. Like being grounded for a week. Or no fast food for a month.

So, in the very sulkiest of voices, Tony said, 'Sorry.'

'Too spoilt is your problem,' said his father. 'Nothing's ever good enough.'

'That's bull,' Tony said under his breath.

'What?' yelled his father.

'Nothing,' said Tony.

'Do you know what, young man?' said his father. 'We're getting sick of your sulky moods. Sick to death of them.'

'Perhaps I should live somewhere else, then,' said Tony.

'Perhaps you should!' said his father. 'Until you wake up to yourself, you can live in the old dunny for all I care.'

'All right, I will,' said Tony.

'Fine,' said his father. 'Good luck.'

Why had Tony said that? How had the argument become so bad so quickly?

Tony knew his mood was much too sooky, much too stubborn, to ever back down, but the dunny? **Poo!**

For those of you who haven't had the pleasure of owning a dunny, it's a toilet that sits in the backyard in a shed. Which is just as well because they usually smell a bit ordinary. They stink is another way of putting it.

Most dunnies were built years ago and some are very old indeed. Sometimes there'd be a flush system with water, but other times they were just a tin can. And now and then, just a big, dark hole. You could never see the bottom of the hole, which is just as well, I guess, as my dad said at the bottom of every hole lived a monster. Still, that never worried me too much – anyone who could live down there was welcome to it.

Luckily for Tony, their dunny (or 'thunderbox', as his dad called it) wasn't in use anymore. But Tony could still think of better places to live.

So, that night after school, Tony shifted out of home and into the dunny.

He could hear his mother in the kitchen saying, 'You can't let him sleep out there. He'll catch his death of cold.'

'Do him good,' said Tony's father. 'Anyway, he'll be back soon enough, with his tail

between his legs.'

Oh no, I won't! thought Tony.

Fortunately, it was rather a large old dunny. *Maybe they made them big to spread the smell,* thought Tony.

In fact, it was so roomy that Tony could almost stretch out on the floor with his head up near the bowl. But then Tony thought of all the thousands of bottoms that had sat only centimetres from his head, and he switched ends.

Really, the whole set-up could almost be described as cosy. Tony had put a blow-up airbed on the floor, followed by a blanket, two sheets, two more blankets, a doona and two pillows.

Not bad, thought Tony. *No worries about a quick visit to the loo during the night, either.*

Earlier, Tony's mum and dad had said they would still cook tea for him but he had to eat it in the dunny. No sweets, either. And tonight was his favourite, chocolate ice-cream.

But just as Tony was about to nod off to sleep, he heard a scraping noise. He flicked on his torch and there, sliding under the door, was a big bowl of ice-cream.

'Is that you, Gary?' whispered Tony.

'Don't tell Dad,' replied Gary.

'Thanks,' said Tony. 'Thanks heaps.'

'What's it like in there?' asked Gary.

'Not too bad. A bit like a cubby house,' said Tony.

'Does it still stink?' asked Gary.

'Yep,' said Tony. 'Look... Sorry I punched you this morning.'

'I wouldn't worry too much,' said Gary. 'I just pinched those lollies from your drawer. And you know all your basketball posters? You should see how excellent they look in my room.'

Tony heard the sound of running feet.

As Tony lay there, he started to wonder, for the first time really, why he got into bad moods. Maybe he was spoilt. Maybe his mum was right when she said that he needed more sleep and that he really should try going to bed earlier.

He knew his parents loved him. And they

weren't that bad — as oldies go, anyway. So what was it? Maybe it was just the way he was. The way he was born.

Whatever, Tony knew it was much too soon to go back into the house. That would be weak. Who knows, it might suit him to never go back.

It so happened that winter was coming on and the next two nights were freezing. A cold wind whistled around the dunny bowl, the door rattled, strange noises seemed to come from every corner and a snail tried to slide into Tony's ear. He caught it just in time by squashing it against his cheek.

Poor Tony. Much as he hated to admit it, he was becoming scared. But there was still

no way he was going back inside the house. Not yet, anyway.

He'd got himself into an awful situation. *What am I going to do?* he thought, shivering. *I'll be stuck out here forever.*

Well, it's a matter of fact that there aren't too many old dunnies left these days. Most of them have burnt down or blown down or just fallen over from old age. And so it was with Tony Boyd's dunny.

The very next day, Tony arrived home to find nothing except a blackened dunny bowl and a pile of ash.

As he stared in amazement, his dad came up from behind, put his hand on Tony's shoulder and said, 'Must have been a spark from next door's chimney.'

'What about my doona and stuff?' asked Tony.

'Got them out just in time,' said his dad. 'They're in your room. Now that the dunny's gone, I thought it might be time to come back inside?'

Tony still hadn't turned around to look his dad in the eye, but he said, 'Yeah, I reckon it might.'

'Mates?' asked his dad.

'Mates,' said Tony.

And with that, Tony turned and gave his

dad the biggest hug they'd had in years.

It might have been a spark that caused the dunny to burn down…or it might also have been a match.

From the box **in Tony's dad's pocket.**

two good girls decide to become naughty

Sally couldn't understand it. Lately, she seemed to be hungry all the time. Always going to the fridge. Always dreaming of food.

Then Jenny, her sister, said something too. 'I'm so hungry I could eat a horse and chase the jockey.'

Jenny, whose usual idea of pigging out was a glass of water and a deep breath!

'What do you think it is?' asked Sal.

Jenny didn't know. Perhaps it was like Dad said, that they were both just growing girls? Perhaps.

But going to the kitchen and actually making a snack for themselves? Looking in the back of the fridge? Drinking milk? Something had to be wrong.

And then Dad noticed. And Dad wasn't happy. 'Why, may I ask, is there only one muesli bar left for lunches? Three days ago there were six whole boxes!' he yelled.

Jenny and Sal hung their heads in shame and said nothing. For a very good reason.

They knew if they kept quiet then sooner or later, Dad would stop. And later on still, he'd say sorry for yelling at them and tell them he loved them and ask for a cuddle. It worked every time.

'Don't I feed you enough?' shouted Dad. 'I've bought bigger lunch boxes, I'm having trouble squeezing the lid on because I put in so much – and still it's not enough!'

Sal couldn't help herself. This time she had to say something.

'I don't understand,' said Sal. 'I reckon you've been giving us less!'

'Less!' roared Dad. 'What was it this morning? Two sandwiches, a drink, an apple, a banana, a muesli bar –'

'What sandwiches?' interrupted Jenny.

They all went quiet. Suddenly it all made sense. The fights for the last piece of cake were finally explained. Someone had been stealing their lunches.

Jenny and Sal knew they should leave the whole thing up to their dad. He was absolutely right when he said the best way to handle it would be for him to speak to the teacher. And they knew if they even tried to do something themselves, their dad would crack a wobbly.

But it didn't stop them. Here was a chance to play detective. To catch a thief. Just like on television. Surely being naughty just once couldn't hurt?

Jenny had a plan. First they'd try to find

out who the thief was, grab them after school
and then really tell them off. If *that* didn't
work, they'd secretly put something awful
in their sandwiches. Something that tasted
really, really terrible. Something that would
make a rat chuck. That would teach the thief
a lesson.

Excellent idea, thought Sal, but how?

'Well,' said Jenny, 'whoever it is, they
must be stealing our lunches during playtime.
Because a couple of times we have arrived at
school right on the bell, and then we always
go straight to our bags as soon as lunchtime
starts. When else could it be?'

'Good thinking,' said Sal. 'So if one of us
hides inside during playtime, then we'll be

able to see who it is?'

'Exactly,' said Jenny. Jenny had that same grin she used to get whenever she was planning to tease her sister.

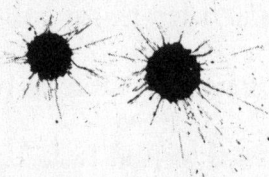

The very next day, Sal hid behind the door and used the windows as a sort of mirror to see who was hanging around their bags.

Suddenly she could hear someone. And then she could *see* someone. And that someone went straight to Sal's bag. Out came her lunch box and into that someone's mouth popped a sandwich. The someone turned around and you'll never guess who it was.

Dirty Darren.

I suppose I'd better tell you first why he was called Dirty Darren. He had the most disgusting habit of letting goobies hang out of his nose. And then he licked them. It always seemed as if Darren needed to blow his nose. But he never did. He just licked. Filthy, dirty, disgusting Darren.

So Jenny grabbed Darren after school and said, 'We know.'

'Know what?' said Darren.

'We've seen you!' said Jenny. 'Pinching our lunches.'

'So what?' replied Darren. 'Finders keepers.'

'Finders keepers?' yelled Jenny.

'Yeah,' said Darren. 'I used to look in all the girls' lunch boxes. But your sandwiches are always the best.'

Jenny could feel herself getting really angry. She couldn't help asking, 'Why only girls?'

'Because girls are stupid. And weak,' replied Darren. 'What are girls going to do about it?'

Well, you can imagine how Jenny felt after that. She was so mad she thought she would burst. But do you know what? She didn't say anything. She just turned and left.

'Good on you for walking away,' said Sally, back at their house. 'Like Dad says, it's no use

fighting. Just makes you as bad as they are.'

'Bad?' said Jenny. 'I'm going back to our plan of putting something in our sandwiches, and I tell you what, it's going to be the worst, filthiest, stinkiest mixture you can think of. Darren's going to wish he'd never even heard of lunch.'

First, Jenny found some cat poo.

They didn't have to pick it up with their hands because they used Dad's kitchen tongs. Then they got some ash from the fireplace,

some scraps from the compost heap and then they threw in a pair of Dad's undies. Finally, they added milk

and dog food and then let the whole lot sit in the sun for a week.

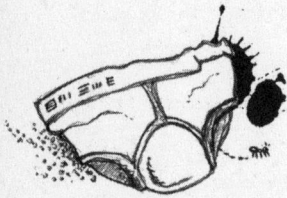

Well, you can imagine what it was like after *that*. It was the worst-smelling

sort of cheesy stuff you could ever imagine. Just to spread it into the sandwiches, Sal had to pinch her nose shut.

They took the secret sandwiches to school, hid behind the door and waited. Sure enough,

Darren crept up and checked to see no-one was watching. He had a particularly large gooby that day – so large, in fact, that Sal and Jenny could see it in the window they used as a mirror.

Darren took out the sandwiches, opened his mouth and took **the biggest bite** you'll ever see. The girls held their breath and waited.

Darren chewed, and thought about the taste, and chewed again, and thought again. And do you know what he said?

'Excellent.'

And as he spoke, that very large gooby rolled out of his nose and onto the sandwich. Right onto the corner from which Darren took his next large bite.

'Rad,' said Darren.

The girls just couldn't believe it. Dirty, filthy, disgusting Darren thought they were the best sandwiches he'd ever tasted! The girls' heads dropped with disappointment. Sometimes life's just not fair.

It's funny how things have a way of catching up with people, though. You see, Darren eventually got sick of stealing lunches. Somehow it wasn't funny anymore. And besides, he'd found something else to do. Chase after Kelly Lipton.

Darren had decided he liked girls after all, and he especially liked Kelly Lipton. But Kelly wasn't so sure about Darren. She couldn't decide if he was handsome and funny, or a real dork.

Well, one day, Darren organised this game of kiss chasey. You can guess who he chased! And he caught her.

But just when he asked if he could give Kelly a little kiss on the cheek, this huge gooby appeared. **A monster.**

It slid out of his nose and sat trembling on his lip.

I don't think you'll have too much trouble guessing what Kelly's answer was. And that's not all she said. I've promised not to tell, but let's just say it wasn't very nice. And straight after, Jenny and Sal started telling a joke.

'What's the difference between kissing Darren and putting your head in a bucket full of goobies? The bucket.'

The joke went around for ages and Darren was really upset. What a shame.

These days, Darren carries a hanky. And he spends a lot of time checking himself in the mirror. Instead of feeling tough in front of girls, I think he's just a little bit scared of them.

And so he should be.

Are you ready for some more SHOCKING stories?

Naughty STORIES for Good boys and girls

CHRISTOPHER·MILNE

the day your teacher went Mad AND OTHER Naughty STORIES for Good boys and girls CHRISTOPHER·MILNE

THE BRAVEST KID I've ever known AND OTHER Naughty STORIES for Good boys and girls CHRISTOPHER·MILNE

the girl who blew up her brother AND OTHER Naughty STORIES for Good boys and girls CHRISTOPHER·MILNE

available from all good bookshops

www.ChristopherMilne.com.au

hardie grant EGMONT

ABOUT THE AUTHOR

When successful actor and screenwriter
Christopher Milne became a father, he found
himself reading books at bedtime to his two boys,
Peter and Robert. He soon ran out of stories
to read, so he started making up his own.

He quickly discovered that if he told Pete and Rob
about good boys and girls doing very good things
all the time, they were bored stupid.

But if he told them about naughty kids doing **pooey,
rotten, disgusting** things, his sons would scream for
more. 'We want more of those naughty stories!'

'OK,' Chris would reply. 'But only if you've been good.'
And so the **Naughty Stories for Good Boys and Girls**
were born...

For more info on Christopher Milne and his books, go to

www.ChristopherMilne.com.au